E   Stevenson, James
St   The worst person in the
            world
           cl

"Party?" said the children.

"Party?" said Ugly.

"Don't stand there dawdling," said the worst,
  and he marched off down the street
  with Ugly and the children
  running along behind.

"No, you can't," said the worst.

"We can't?" said Timmy. "Why not?"

"Because if you do," said the worst,

"then all the ice cream will melt,

and the party will be ruined."

Suddenly, there was a rustling in the bushes
and out came the worst person. He was wearing
a striped party hat, and in his hand he held
the baseball. "Is this yours?" he called.
The children cheered.
The worst gave the ball to Ugly. "Thanks,"
said Ugly. "Now we can finish the game."

"That ball is gone," said Celeste.
"We'll never find it now," said Tony.
"I guess the game is over."

In the field down the street, Timmy was at bat
and Celeste was pitching. "Strike two!" yelled Ugly.
Celeste wound up and threw the next pitch.
Timmy swung as hard as he could. Crack!

The ball sailed up and across the field and fell
into some trees and bushes near the street.
"Home run!" cried Ugly.

In a dark corner, behind a pile of dishes, he noticed a striped party hat. "Imagine wearing one of those things," he said. "I would have looked like a fool." Then he thought, Of course everybody else would have been wearing one too.

He picked up the hat and went over to an old, cracked mirror. Slowly, he put the hat on his head. "Hmmm," he said.

The worst went into the living room and put on a record.
It sounded awful. He turned it off.

He looked around the kitchen.
"I better get used to this again," he said.
"This is the way it's always going to be . . . "

After a long time, he got up and went downstairs.
The party decorations were all gone.
Ugly had put everything back the way it was before.
The house was dark and messy. In the kitchen,
the ice cream was melting in the sink.

He sat in his room. For a while he could hear
Ugly moving around downstairs, and then
he heard Ugly and the children playing
baseball far away down the street.
They were laughing and shouting.
The worst put his hands over his ears.

"Gee, I would have asked you what you wanted,
   but you were asleep," said Ugly.
"I'll tell you what I want," said the worst.
"I want no party, no baseball, no children,
   and no <u>you</u>! Goodbye!"
And he went upstairs.

The worst went into the house.

"How do you like the decorations?" said Ugly,
   following him in.

"I hate the decorations," said the worst.

"I hate the balloons, I hate the ice cream,
   I hate the cake, the favors, the plates,
   the hats, and everything else."

Ugly and Timmy and Celeste and Tony arrived,
carrying baseball gloves.

"What's this?" said the worst.

"First we're having a baseball game, then
the party," said Ugly. "That way, everybody
will work up an appetite."

He went downstairs. "Oh, <u>no</u>," he said.
The whole downstairs was decorated for a party.

Late the next morning, when the worst got up,
the house was silent. "Ha," said the worst.
"That creature has gone away."

The worst person went to bed, but the noise
of snoring filled the house and kept him awake.
"Invitations?" he said. "Shebang?"…
It was nearly dawn when he finally got to sleep.

At the end of the day, the lawn was all cleared.

"I'm pooped," said Ugly. "Mind if I get some shut-eye?"

"There's no place for you to sleep," said the worst.

"Please don't go to any trouble," said Ugly.

"I can sleep anywhere."

He flopped down on the floor.

"You get started on the invitations for tomorrow,"
he said. "See you in the morning."

Then he began to snore.

"Now the lawn," he said and went outside.

"Stop doing that!" yelled the worst.

"Don't worry!" called Ugly.

"I don't get poison ivy."

He washed the dishes.   He swept the floors,

and cleaned the windows.

"Oh, nothing fancy," said Ugly, grabbing a rag and brushing away some cobwebs. "A little ice cream, balloons, favors, cake..."
"Not in my house," said the worst.

Ugly gathered the dishes that were piled around the house.
"What are you doing?" said the worst.
"Getting ready for the big shebang!" said Ugly.

"You know what?" said Ugly. "If we got this dump cleaned up, we could invite a lot of people over and have a pretty good party."

"People?" said the worst. "Party?"

Ugly went into the kitchen. "You've got lots
of lemons!" he said.
"Don't take too many," said the worst.
Ugly popped three lemons into his mouth.
There was a loud crunch and then he drank
a glass of water. "Delicious!" he said.

They came to the worst person's house.

"You certainly have a terrible-looking place,"
   said Ugly.

"Watch out for the poison ivy,"
   said the worst.

"I'm parched," said Ugly. "Do you happen to know
    where I could find a little lemonade?"
"No," said the worst.
"Don't you have any lemons at your house?" asked Ugly.
"I'm not sure," said the worst.
"Well, let's go take a look!" said Ugly. "Lead the way!"

"You certainly are ugly," said the worst.
"Oh, I know," said Ugly, "but if you've got
   a pleasing personality that's all that counts."
"Rubbish!" said the worst.

He stood up and saw a large creature.

"Howdy," said the creature.

"Who are you?" demanded the worst person.

"I'm the ugliest thing in the world," said
the creature, "but just call me Ugly."

He went into the woods. Birds were singing in the trees.
He told them to shush.

He sat down under a big tree. He thought he was alone,
but then he heard something moving.

His neighbors were standing on the sidewalk, smiling and talking.
He turned off into a field so he wouldn't meet them.

Timmy and Tony and Celeste were searching for their baseball
in the tall grass.
"Have you seen our ball, Mr. Worst?" asked Timmy.
"Certainly not," he said, looking right at it.

One morning the worst person got up and looked outside.
It was a beautiful day. "If there's anything I hate it's spring,"
he said and pulled down the shade.

He ate a lemon for breakfast.
"Ugh," he said. "Too sweet."

He went out for a walk and
hit flowers with his umbrella.

He lived all alone in a terrible mess. Most of the day he sat in a very uncomfortable chair and listened to old records he didn't like.

Some of the time he watched from a window so that if anybody came near his house he could yell, "Go away!" (But nobody ever came near <u>his</u> house.)

In an old house in a yard full of poison ivy
lived the worst person in the world.

Designed by Ava Weiss

1   2   3   4   5   6   7   8   9   10

The text is set in ITC Zapf International Medium.
The display type is Typositor Grumpy.

Library of Congress Cataloging in Publication Data

Stevenson, James (date) The worst person in the world.
SUMMARY: The meeting of the worst person in the world and the ugliest
person in the world has some unexpected results. (1.   Friendship—Fiction)
I.   Title.   PZ7.S84748Wo   (E)   77-22141   ISBN 0-688-80127-7
ISBN 0-688-84127-9 lib. bdg.

The Worst Person
in the World

by JAMES STEVENSON

GREENWILLOW BOOKS

A Division of William Morrow & Company, Inc. • New York